For Marjorie Denise Dance, and our ancestors
Arielle

To all my grandchildren, and grandchildren everywhere
Jenny

First published in the United Kingdom in 2022 by Lantana Publishing Ltd.
www.lantanapublishing.com | info@lantanapublishing.com

American edition published in 2022 by Lantana Publishing Ltd., UK.

Text © Arielle Dance, 2022
Illustration © Jenny Duke, 2022

Distributed in the United States and Canada by Lerner Publishing Group, Inc.
241 First Avenue North, Minneapolis, MN 55401 U.S.A.
For reading levels and more information, look for this title at www.lernerbooks.com
Cataloging-in-Publication Data Available.

Hardback ISBN: 978-1-913747-80-0
eBook PDF: 978-1-913747-81-7
ePub3: 978-1-913747-82-4

Printed and bound in Europe
Original artwork created using mixed media, completed digitally

DEAREST ONE

Arielle Dance

 Lantana

Jenny Duke

Dare to smile

Share a smile with someone you love
or with a stranger in need of a friend.

Your smile can make someone's day
and maybe even change someone's life.

Embrace the rain

Remember that rain is not always gloomy but helps the seeds you have planted grow into tall trees.

So, splash, splash, splash and look for the rainbow!

Find music in the quiet

The wind will breathe a song for you and bring you comfort. The water will make you want to dance.

Dancing is our soul's way of expressing feelings without words. So, keep dancing, every day!

Turn your face to the sun

Stand tall and proud like a sunflower
and plant kindness wherever you go.

A seed of kindness can last a lifetime
and will grow long after you are gone.

Show yourself love

We only get one body, so take care of it.
Take time to play. It's not really exercise
if you're having fun!

Eat those fresh things, leafy things,
green things. It will be worth it.

Take up space

Remember to find your magic, even when someone tries to dim your flame.

You are a unicorn, a mermaid, a fairy, a dragon.

You have the power within you to be whoever you are meant to be.

Be brave even when you are scared

Bullies never win. Being unique
is a treasure. Never let anyone
make you feel small.

You are a magical being.

Be gentle with yourself

No one wins every game. Sometimes we lose and that hurts. Be understanding when people fall short. When you mess up, the nicest thing someone can say is, it will be okay.

Remember, it will be okay.

Choose your path

Left or right, right or wrong, to stay or to go?
Your life will be full of choices. There will be
curves and stumbles, but the path you choose
will be the right one because it's yours.

Shine your light

Discover the light inside yourself for all the world to see.

On those dark days, find one thing that brings you joy and reminds you that life is for living!

Remember who you are

You hold the magic of your ancestors within you.
We are with you, guiding your path.

Remember to tell our stories and pass them on.

Know true love

You deserve all the love the universe
can pour out. Keep your heart open and
love will find you right where you are.

Dearest one, you are loved!